蓋爾的生日慶祝會

卡蒂・蒂格

GAIL'S BIRTHDAY PARTY

KATI TEAGUE

叢書編輯：羅斯瑪麗・蘭寧

Series Editor : Rosemary Lanning

Magi Publications, London

Published in 1991 by Magi Publications,
in association with Star Books International, 55 Crowland Avenue, Hayes, Middx UB3 4JP

Printed and bound in Hong Kong.

Translated into Chinese by Chinatech
ISBN 1 85430 231 0

那天是蓋爾的生日。由於太興奮了,她早上很早就醒來,
其他的人還在呼呼大睡呢。

It was Gail's birthday. She was so excited that she woke up really
early. Everyone else was still asleep.

吃早餐時，爸爸給了蓋爾一堆生日卡。她看不懂卡上的所有名字，可是媽媽在幫助她。

At breakfast time Dad brought Gail a pile of birthday cards. She couldn't read all the names in them, but Mum helped her.

"我們還有什麼東西在這裏啊?"爸爸說着打開了櫥櫃,
看到裏邊裝着一些包裹,蓋爾高興得直叫。

"And what have we here?" said Dad, opening a cupboard to
reveal some parcels. Gail squealed with delight.

這是爸爸，媽媽給她的禮物－幾件漂亮嶄新的衣服。
"我現在就穿上試試看！"蓋爾說。

It was a present from Mum and Dad – some lovely bright new
clothes. "I'm going to try them on right now!" said Gail.

小傑克也要開包裹。在他撕去包裝紙時抿嘴直笑。

Baby Jack wanted to open a parcel, too. He chuckled as he ripped the paper off.

"準備你的派對還要做好多事呢，"爸爸說：
"從那裏開始呢？先吹氣球？"

"There's lots to do to get your party ready," said Dad. "Where shall we start? With the balloons?"

蓋爾一口氣，一口氣地吹着，但是她不能使她的氣球大起來。爸爸笑着說：" 你可以用氣筒麼。"

Gail puffed and puffed, but she couldn't get her balloon to blow up. "You can use the pump," laughed Dad.

剛過中午，媽媽把蓋爾叫上樓。她不知道爲什麼，
但一看媽媽的臉色就知道是有甚麼秘密。

Early in the afternoon Mum called Gail upstairs. She wouldn't say
why, but she had a look on her face that meant secrets.

蓋爾在納悶，樓上根本沒甚麼東西。所以她轉身跑回廚房。
"先不要進來！"爸爸說："不然你要掃興的。"

Gail was puzzled. There was nothing to see upstairs. So she
rushed back to the kitchen. "Don't come in yet!" said Dad.
"You'll spoil the surprise."

門鈴大聲地響着。原來是利亞姆，他看上去很時髦，
手裏拿着個大包裹。

The doorbell rang loudly. It was Liam. He looked very smart and
was carrying a big parcel.

接着，許多人也來了。安娜與她爸爸和小妹妹一起來了。
"別忘了你的禮品！"安娜的爸爸說。

After that, lots more people arrived. Anna came with her Dad and baby sister. "Don't forget your present!" said Anna's Dad.

爸爸放起音樂讓大家一起玩。傑克要參加進去，
可是他老是栽跟斗！他使得蓋爾也一起跟着栽。

Dad put on music for musical bumps. Jack wanted to join in, but
he kept falling over! He made Gail fall over, too.

"別讓蓋爾坐下來！"尼克說，"音樂還沒停呢。"
蓋爾想這個並不是很好玩。

"Don't make Gail sit down!" said Nicky. "The music hasn't
stopped." Gail didn't think that was very funny.

" 你們這麼跳上跳下，現在肯定很餓了吧，"媽媽說：
" 吃點心吧！"

"Now, you must be hungry after all that jumping up and down,"
said Mum. "Time for tea!"

有很多好吃的東西，每個人還有一頂派對帽。
蓋爾對自己的尤其喜歡。

There were lots of lovely things to eat and a party hat for each of
the children. Gail was especially pleased with hers.

爸爸端着生日蛋糕進來了，"這就是我們的秘密。"他說。

Then Dad came in with a wonderful birthday cake. "That was the surprise," he said.

他點上蠟燭，蓋爾吹滅它們時，
每個人唱起"祝你生日快樂！"歌。

He lit the candles and everyone sang, "Happy Birthday to you!"
as Gail blew them out.

餘下的時間便是更多的遊戲了。伊姆蘭被蒙上眼睛，
他竭力去抓住其他人。

Then it was time for more games. Imran was blindfolded and had
to try to catch the others.

"現在我們來玩氣球吧，"蓋爾說。每個人都因抓氣球而玩得十分累了，利亞姆這次差一點栽倒。

"Let's play with the balloons now," said Gail. Everyone got very tired trying to catch them and Liam nearly fell over this time.

利亞姆選擇了下一個遊戲，是"捉迷藏"。
利亞姆閉上雙眼開始數十，所有其他人全躲起來。

Liam chose the next game. It was hide and seek. Liam closed his
eyes and counted to ten while everyone else hid.

"我來了！"利亞姆叫着，"躲好啦！"他能聽到從傢俱背後發出的嬉笑聲。

"Coming!" shouted Liam. "Ready or not!" He could hear giggles from behind the furniture.

不久客人都該回家了。安娜的爸爸來接安娜，伊姆蘭和
利亞姆。他們每人都帶一片蛋糕和一個氣球回家。

Soon it was time to go home. Anna's Dad came to collect
Anna, Imran and Liam. They all took home a piece of cake
and a balloon.

蓋爾幫媽媽和爸爸收拾。氣球，飄帶到處都是。

Gail helped Mum and Dad tidy up. There were balloons and
streamers everywhere.

" 這次是我所有的生日中最好的一個。" 蓋爾上牀時說，
她立刻就進入了夢鄉。

"This was the best birthday ever," said Gail when she went to bed,
and she fell asleep at once.

Playbooks

Picture books   23 x 20cm, 32 pages

Imran's Clinic
Imran's baby brother needs his
injections, so after a visit to the real
doctor, Imran and the others set
about creating their own surgery in
Anna's bedroom!

Liam's Day Out
Liam's parents take the four
youngsters on a visit to a farm. Being
an urban child, Liam is rather
apprehensive at first, but he soon
finds things to enjoy in the
countryside.

Anna Goes to School
It is time for Anna to start school, and
she's not too keen, but after her first
day there, she's ready for more.

Gail's Birthday
Mum and Dad and baby brother,
Jack, all contribute to the fun on
Gail's special day.

These titles are available in English only and in the following dual-language editions
(with English): Bengali, Chinese, Greek, Gujarati, Hindi, Punjabi, Turkish, Urdu,
Vietnamese.

Board books   15 x 15cm, 12 pages

Getting Dressed
Shows how and how not to do it.

Faces
Including happy, clean, dirty and
masked ones.

Opposites
Near and far, sweet and sour, and
others.

Arms & Legs
How they help us play and run.

'Delightful books which will certainly encourage the young child to behave as a
reader.'   *School Librarian*

'These books offer excellent opportunities for learning and conversation in company
with an adult.'   *Contact (PPA Magazine)*

These titles are available in English only and French only and in the following
dual-language editions (with English): Armenian, Bengali, Chinese, Estonian,
French, German, Gujarati, Hebrew, Hindi, Hungarian, Italian, Japanese, Latvian,
Lithuanian, Polish, Portuguese, Punjabi, Spanish, Ukrainian, Urdu, Vietnamese.

Best-selling Magi dual-language picture books

Naughty Bini   Mamta Bhatia and Keir Wickenham

Happy Birthday Bini   Mamta Bhatia and Anna Louise

Grandmother's Tale   Moy McCrory and Eleni Michael

A Country Far Away   Nigel Gray and Philippe Dupasquier

Purnima's Parrot   Feroza Mathieson and Anna Louise

Sometimes . . .   Anna Louise

The Boy Who Cried Wolf   Tony Ross

Anita and the Magician   Swaran Chandan and Keir Wickenham

A Brother for Celia   Maria Martinez i Vendrell and Roser Capdevila

After Dark   Maria Martinez i Vendrell and Roser Capdevila

Ben's Baby   Michael Foreman

Mum's Strike   Marieluise Ritter, Leonard Ritter and Leon Piesowocki

Amar's Last Wish   Parvez Akhtar and Keir Wickenham

Brush and Chase   Eileen Cadman and Keir Wickenham

The Eagle that Would not Fly   James Aggrey and Wolf Erlbruch

Hello Bump   (Flap book)   Christopher James and Steve Augarde

Bump Sings a Song   (Flap book)   Christopher James and Steve Augarde

Bump in the Park   (Flap book)   Christopher James and Steve Augarde

Bump at the Beach   (Flap book)   Christopher James and Steve Augarde

Bump is Busy   (Board book)   Christopher James and Steve Augarde

Look at Bump   (Board book)   Christopher James and Steve Augarde

Here is Bump   (Board book)   Christopher James and Steve Augarde

Bump at Play   (Board book)   Christopher James and Steve Augarde

All these Magi dual-language books are available in English only and in Bengali, Gujarati, Hindi, Punjabi and Urdu with English. Some titles are also available in Chinese, Greek and Vietnamese with English.